Peter Schlemihl

Adelbert von Chamisso

Translated by Leopold von Loewenstein-Wertheim

ONEWORLD
CLASSICS

ONEWORLD CLASSICS LTD
London House
243-253 Lower Mortlake Road
Richmond
Surrey TW9 2LL
United Kingdom
www.oneworldclassics.com

Peter Schlemihl first published in German in 1813

First published by John Calder (Publishers) Limited in 1957
Translation © John Calder (Publishers) Limited, 1957
This edition first published by Oneworld Classics Limited in 2008
Reprinted 2011

Front cover image © Corbis

Printed in Great Britain by CPI Cox & Wyman Ltd, Reading

ISBN: 978-1-84749-080-3

Contents

Introduction

Louis charles adelaide de Chamisso de Boncourt – as a German he called himself Adelbert von Chamisso – was born at the Château of Boncourt in the Champagne on 27th January 1781. In 1790 his family was forced to flee from the terrors of the French Revolution, in which the ancestral castle was destroyed. They went as exiles first to Liege and subsequently to Aachen, The Hague, Düsseldorf and Southern Germany, finally settling in Berlin in 1796. Henceforth Berlin was to remain Chamisso's home and Germany his spiritual fatherland. He studied at the French Lycée (Französische Gymnasium) in Berlin and became a page to the Queen at the court of Frederick William II. In 1798 he enlisted as an ensign in the Prussian army and in 1801 became a lieutenant.

He hated military life and suffered from poverty and loneliness. After a short visit to France in 1803, he returned to Berlin where, together with friends, among them his compatriot De la Foye, the poet Fouqué and his future biographer J.E. Hitzig, he formed a literary circle which published a magazine (1804–1806) devoted to poetry, to which Chamisso contributed sonnets and other poems. It was his aim to become a German poet but at the same time he followed his scientific bent and spent his leisure hours earnestly pursuing his studies.

Meanwhile war had broken out again with France, which forced Chamisso to take up arms against his own country, though he spent most of the campaign in Hameln, taking part in the humiliating surrender of that fortress to the French. During those years he was busy on a number of poetic works, among them *Adelbert's Fable*, an allegory of his own life, as well as a fairytale, *Fortunatus*, both of which remained unfinished. After the surrender of Hameln, he was allowed to go to France, where he lived unmolested until the peace treaty of Tilsit in 1807, when he returned to Prussia. In 1809 he was honourably discharged from the Prussian army with the rank of captain. A small private income, which he supplemented by teaching, enabled him to resume his studies, though with no clear idea as to his ultimate aims. In 1810, very much against his own inclination, he went to France where his family had arranged a teaching post for him at the Lycée in Napoleonville.

He remained in France for two and a half years, trying in vain to take root there. This is the time in which Chamisso found himself, as he put it, without a shadow – that is to say, without established or recognized background, a born Frenchman, a former Prussian officer, an exile in his own homeland – a sorry figure, a "Schlemihl". In Paris, he formed a romantic attachment with Madame de Staël, in whose literary circle he met Alexander von Humboldt and August Wilhelm Schlegel, whose lectures on literature he translated into French. He finally reached the decision that his destiny lay in Germany and in a scientific career. He returned to Berlin in 1812 and took up the study of anatomy and zoology.

The year 1813, which brought the culmination of the struggle between Germany and France, was a time of great inner struggle for Chamisso. Though a German patriot, he was a Frenchman and felt he could not take up arms once more against France. From this conflict of loyalties the book *Peter Schlemihl* sprang, written as a fairytale for the children of his friend, Hitzig. The Jewish word "Schlemihl" means an unlucky, ridiculous person. This is how Chamisso saw himself at the time. He has described how the idea first came to him: "On a journey I had lost my hat, my portmanteau, gloves, handkerchief – in short, my entire personal effects. Fouqué asked me if I had not also lost my shadow and we both tried to imagine the misfortune of such a loss." And so the idea of the lost shadow came to stand in Chamisso's mind as a symbol for a man without recognized background and connections. "I am nowhere at home," he once wrote to Madame de Staël, "I am a Frenchman in Germany and a German in France. A Catholic among Protestants, a Protestant among Catholics, a Jacobin among aristocrats, an aristocrat among democrats." He was convinced that he was condemned to remain a man without a home, despised and even persecuted.

The world of science and of learning was the only one which had no national barriers and in which he could roam freely.

In 1815 he joined the Russian brig *Rurik*, commanded by Otto von Kotzebue, on a journey of scientific exploration for the Russian Government. The ship put to sea at Copenhagen in July 1815 and in the three years that followed circumnavigated the globe, returning to Swinemünde in the autumn of 1818. Chamisso has given a complete account of this journey, in the course of which he collected a considerable amount of knowledge of the natural sciences, ethnography and languages and brought back a number of valuable specimens of plant and animal life.

Returned to Germany, he devoted himself to science and poetry. He became custodian of the Botanical Gardens in Berlin. He was given the honorary degree of Doctor of Berlin University and finally was made a member of the Berlin Academy of Science. In 1819 he married Antonia Piaste, a young girl of nineteen, whom he had known when she was still a child. By now he had gained full recognition in the literary and scientific world and could devote his energies to the pursuit of his two main interests. Financially he was helped by a grant from the French Government in compensation for the losses he had sustained during the Revolution.

He had the satisfaction of seeing his work acclaimed and himself regarded as a leading German poet. In 1836 his *Collected Works* appeared in four volumes.

The last years of his life were clouded by illness. His wife died in May 1837 and he only survived her by fifteen months. He died on August 21st, 1838, in Berlin.

L.L.W.

Principal Dates of Chamisso's Life

1781	27th January. Born at Boncourt, France.
1790	Family flees to Germany.
1796	Berlin (enters French Lycée and becomes a page).
1798	Enlists in Prussian Army.
1801	Promoted lieutenant.
1803	Visits France.
1804–1806	Germany. First poems and publication of literary magazine.
1805–1806	War service. Writes *Fortunatus*, *Adelbert's Fable* (published 1807) and other miscellaneous works.
1806–1807	In France.
1807	Returns to Berlin.
1809	Discharged from army.
1810–1812	Lives in France.
1812	Returns to Germany.

1813	*Peter Schlemihl.*
1815–1818	Journey round the world.
1819	Marriage to Antonia Piaste. Honorary Doctor of Berlin University.
1821	Publication of *Journey round the World* (revised edition 1836).
1826–1837	Main period of poetic and scientific output.
1831	First *Collected Edition.*
1835	Second enlarged and revised edition of *Works.* Became member of Berlin Academy of Science.
1836	Final edition of *Works* in four volumes.
1838	21st August. Death in Berlin.

Peter Schlemihl

1

A SAFE VOYAGE, but I cannot pretend a pleasant one and now at last we were in port. As soon as we had been put ashore, I picked up my modest luggage, pushing my way through the milling crowd, made for the humblest house I could see with the sign of an inn outside. I asked for a room. The boots gave me one look and sent me to the garret. I demanded some clean water and asked where Mr Thomas John lived. Outside the town, I was told, beyond the North Gate; the first country house on the right – a large new building of red and white marble, with many pillars.

It was still early in the day; I opened my bundle, took out my newly-turned black coat, washed and dressed myself in my best clothes. Then, with my letter of introduction in my pocket, I set out on my way to the man who, I hoped, would further my modest ambitions.

Going up the long North Street, I reached the gate whence I could see the pillars of the squire's country seat gleaming through the trees. Here we are at last, I said to myself. I wiped the dust from my boots with my handkerchief, and straightened my cravat. In God's name, I muttered and resolutely pulled the handle of the bell. The door flew open. In the hall I was subjected to close questioning before the porter would consent to announce me. Thereupon he was good enough to summon me into the park, where Mr John was strolling with a few of his friends. I recognized him at once by his portly, self-complacent air. He received me well enough – as a rich man receives a poor devil – condescending even to look at me (without, however, turning away from his guests) and took the letter of introduction which I held out to him.

"Well, well," he said, "fancy a letter from my brother! I have not heard from him for a long time. I trust he is in good health? Over there," he continued, addressing himself to the assembled company without waiting for my reply and pointing with the letter to a hillock, "over there I am putting up a new building." He then broke the seal of the letter, without interrupting the conversation, which seemed to turn on the subject of wealth. "In my considered opinion," he exclaimed, "a man who is worth less than a million is, if you will pardon the expression, a ragamuffin."

"How very true!" I hastened to concur with deep feeling. This must have pleased him for he smiled.

"Stay here, my young friend; I may have time later to tell you what I think of it," he said, indicating the letter, which he put into his pocket. He then turned again towards the company and offered his arm to a young lady; most of the other gentlemen followed his example, pairing off with the ladies of their choice, and the whole party made towards the rose-covered hill.

I lingered behind, not wishing to impose my presence – an unnecessary precaution, for no one took the slightest notice of me. The company seemed in high spirits. There was much joking and flirting and the ponderous discussion of trifles, while serious matters were dismissed with levity. In the main, the shafts of their witticisms were directed at

absent friends and their affairs. I was too much of a
stranger to make anything of their conversation, too
engrossed in my own business to take an interest in
their badinage.

We had reached the rose grove. The lovely Fanny,
who seemed to be the girl of the moment, insisted
on breaking off a flowering branch; she pricked
herself with a thorn and blood, so red that it might
have come from the roses themselves, flowed over
her delicate hand. The incident caused a lively
commotion and someone called for a dressing. A
quiet elderly man, tall and rather thin, whom I had
not previously noticed, instantly put his hand into
the close-fitting coat-tail pocket of his old-fashioned
grey taffeta coat and produced a small wallet,
from which he took some sticking-plaster which
he handed to the lady with a courteous bow. She
received it without so much as a nod of thanks. The
small scratch was duly bound up and the company
proceeded to the brow of the hill, from which they
wished to enjoy the magnificent view over the green
labyrinth of the park and the infinite expanse of the
sea beyond.

It was indeed a grand and noble sight. A light speck appeared on the horizon between the dark blue waters and the azure of the sky.

"Bring a telescope," called Mr John, and before any of the servants answering the call had bestirred themselves, the man in grey had already put his hand into his coat pocket and produced a beautiful *Dolland* which, with a modest bow, he handed to the Squire. The latter immediately raised it to his eye and informed the company that what he saw was the ship which had sailed yesterday and was held by contrary winds outside the port.

The telescope passed from hand to hand, but was not returned to the owner. I looked at him in astonishment, unable to understand how this large instrument could have come out of so small a pocket. No one else showed any surprise and no one appeared to pay any more attention to the man in grey than to myself.

Refreshments were served, the choicest fruits of many lands piled up on precious plates. Mr John did the honours with easy grace and for the second time addressed me.

"Eat your fill, young man. I'm sure you've had very little to eat during your voyage." I bowed to him, but he was already talking to someone else.

It soon appeared that it was the wish of the company to rest awhile on the slope of the hill facing the broad sweep of the landscape below: unfortunately, the grass was too damp. It would be divine, someone suggested, if Turkish rugs could be spread on the ground. Hardly had the wish been expressed than the man in grey put his hand in his pocket and with a modest, even humble, gesture, produced a gorgeous carpet, woven with gold. The servants took it from him as though this were nothing unusual and spread it on the selected spot and, without further ado, the company settled down on it. I looked with consternation at the man, his pocket and then at the carpet, which measured twenty paces in length and ten in width. I rubbed my eyes, not knowing what to think, especially as no one else appeared to see anything remarkable in what had just occurred.

I longed to know more about the man, to find out who he was but I did not know whom to ask, for I was almost more afraid of the haughty servants than of their haughty masters. At last I mustered my courage and went up to a young man who, I concluded, was socially not quite equal to the others, for he was mostly left standing by himself. I asked him in a low voice who the obliging gentleman in grey might be.

"You mean the one who looks like a bit of thread blown away from a tailor's needle?"

"Yes, the one standing over there alone."

"I don't know him," he replied and, obviously not too keen to enter into discussion with me, he turned away and started a trivial conversation with someone.

The sun was now blazing down, which seemed to be distressing the ladies. The delightful Fanny nonchalantly turned to the man in grey whom, as far as I know, no one had hitherto addressed, and frivolously asked him if by any chance he could oblige with a marquee. He acknowledged the request by a deep bow, as if to express that this was indeed an undeserved honour, and at once put his hand into his pocket, extracting canvas pegs, ropes and framework; in short, everything with which to erect a most sumptuous tent. The young bloods helped him to put it up; it covered the whole extent of the carpet, and again, no one seemed to consider the incident as at all extraordinary. To me all this was becoming increasingly uncanny, indeed quite horrifying, and my dismay was complete when, on the next wish casually expressed by somebody, the man in grey produced from his pocket three horses – I repeat, three magnificent black steeds, saddled and bridled. Just imagine, three saddled horses from the same pocket from which he had already produced a wallet, a telescope, a large woven carpet and a pleasure tent, complete in every respect, to fit over the carpet! If I did not solemnly swear that I have seen it all with my own eyes, I am sure you could not believe it. Despite the man's obvious embarrassment and humility, and the fact that no one seemed to pay much attention to him, his ghostly figure, at which I stared with fascination, had something so appallingly sinister that I could bear it no longer.

I decided to steal away from the company, which seemed to be easy enough considering the insignificant part I had been playing. I wanted to return to the city and try my luck once more the following day with Mr John, and perhaps if I could muster up sufficient courage, ask him about the man in grey. Oh, if only I had made my escape then and there! I had managed to leave the rose grove unobserved and to reach an open lawn at the bottom of the hill when, apprehensive at the thought that I might be observed straying off the gravel path, I stopped to look round. I was startled to see the man in grey walking towards me. He raised his hat and bowed to me more deeply than anyone had ever done. There was no doubt that he wished to speak to me, and without being extremely rude it was impossible to avoid him. I, too, took off my hat and bowed to him, and there I stood rooted to the soil in the blazing sun. I trembled with fear as I looked at him; I felt like a bird hypnotized by a snake. He himself seemed to be embarrassed; he did not raise his eyes, repeatedly bowed to me and then, coming quite close, spoke in a low and uncertain voice like someone asking for alms.

"Will the gentleman pardon my importunity if I presume to speak to him without having been formally introduced. I have a request to make if you will kindly—"

"For Heaven's sake, dear sir," I broke in with apprehension, "what can I do for a man who..." We both stopped short and both seemed to blush.

After a moment's silence he resumed:

"In the short time in which I had the good fortune to find myself in your presence I have, my dear sir, repeatedly – if you will permit me to say so – observed with truly inexpressible admiration the magnificent shadow which you, standing in the sun, with a certain noble contempt and without being aware of it, cast from you – this wonderful shadow there at your feet. Forgive this truly daring imposition but would you not perhaps consider disposing of your shadow?"

I was silent, my head in a whirl. What was I to make of this strange request to buy my shadow? He must be crazy, I thought, and in a tone that contrasted forcibly with the humility of his own I answered:

"Come, come, my good friend, will not your own shadow do? This seems a deal of a most unusual kind."

He quickly continued. "I have," he said, "in my pocket many things which might not appear unacceptable to the gentleman; for this invaluable shadow no price can be high enough."

A chill crept up my spine because that sinister pocket came to my mind and I could not think why I had addressed him as my good friend. I spoke again and tried to get out of my predicament with exquisite politeness.

"Sir, if you will forgive your most humble servant I am not able to grasp the meaning of your proposal; how could I possibly part with my shadow—"

He interrupted me. "I only crave for your permission to lift up your noble shadow right here and to put it into my pocket; how I do it is my own affair. In return, and as a token of my profound gratitude to the gentleman, I will leave him to make his choice among all the treasures which I carry in my pocket. The genuine mandrake root, magic pennies, robber's ducat, the magic napkin of Roland's Knights, the gallows mandrake; but all this may not be of sufficient interest to you. I have something much better: Fortunatus' wishing cap restored as new and also a lucky purse exactly like the one he possessed."

"Fortunatus' lucky purse!" I interrupted, for, great as had been my fear, his words captured my imagination. I felt quite dizzy and double ducats sparkled before my eyes.

"Will the gentleman deign to inspect and try out this purse." He put his hand into his pocket and produced a firmly stitched leather purse of moderate size with two strong leather strings and handed it to me. I dipped into it and took out ten pieces of gold and ten more, ten more and yet another ten. I quickly held out my hand to him and said:

"Done, the deal is on. For this purse you may have my shadow."

We shook hands on it, he knelt down and I watched him as, with astounding dexterity, he silently detached my shadow from head to foot from the lawn. He lifted it up, carefully folded it and finally put it into his pocket. He then stood up, bowed deeply and withdrew to the rose grove. I thought I heard him softly laughing to himself. I firmly held the purse by its strings – the sun was shining brightly around me – as I stood there dazed by what had happened.

2

WHEN AT LAST I had recovered my senses I hastened away from the place, wishing to be rid of it once and for all. I filled my pockets with the gold and concealed the purse under my coat, fastening the strings firmly round my neck. I left the park unnoticed, reached the highroad and made my way to the city. Engrossed in my own thoughts, I approached the gates, when I heard someone calling behind me.

"Young man! Hey, young man, listen to me!" I turned round and saw an old woman shouting after me. "Look out, sir, you have lost your shadow."

"Many thanks, my good woman." I replied, throwing a gold piece for the well-meant cautioning, and stepped into the shade of the trees.

At the gate the sentry challenged me: "Where has the gentleman left his shadow?" and immediately afterwards a couple of women exclaimed: "Good

Heavens, the poor fellow has no shadow." I began to be annoyed and I carefully avoided walking in the sun. This, unfortunately, I could not do all the time; for instance, not when crossing the High Street which, as ill luck would have it, I had to do at the very moment when the boys were coming out of school. One of them, a cheeky, hunchbacked little rascal, immediately saw that my shadow was missing. With much hilarity, he informed the whole gang of young hooligans, who now gave chase, making fun and throwing mud at me. "Decent people take their shadows with them when walking in the sun!" they shouted. Finally, I had to scatter handfuls of gold among them to get rid of them and jumped into a hackney carriage with the help of some charitable onlookers. As soon as I found myself alone in the cab, I burst into tears. It was already beginning to dawn upon me that even as gold on this earth is more highly esteemed than merit and virtue, so the shadow might be more highly esteemed even than gold; and that as I had previously held my conscience higher than wealth, I had now given up my shadow for the sake of gold; what on earth could, what ought to become of me?

I was still greatly upset when the carriage set me down at my old inn. I could not bear the idea of returning to my miserable garret. I had my things brought down, received my pitiful bundle with a gesture of contempt, threw down a few ducats on the counter and then ordered the carriage to take me to the best hotel in town. It faced north, so I had nothing to fear from the sun. I dismissed the driver with gold, selected the best front room and shut myself up in it immediately.

And what do you think I did? Oh, my dear Chamisso, it makes me blush to confess it even to you. I pulled out the cursed purse from underneath my coat and in a kind of frenzy, which burned me up like a conflagration, I extracted gold from it; more and more gold, which I scattered over the floor. I trampled on it, making it tinkle and feasting my senses on its glitter and sound; I piled gold upon gold till I sank exhausted onto my luxurious bed, wallowing in a yellow flood. Thus the day went by and the evening. I did not open my door, and when night finally came, I fell asleep embedded in gold.

29

Then I dreamt of you. I dreamt I was standing outside the glass door of your little study and saw you sitting at your desk between a skeleton and a bunch of dried plants. Before you, volumes of Haller, Humboldt and Linée lay open on the desk, and on the sofa there was a volume of Goethe and the Magic Ring. I looked at you for a long time and looked at every object in the room; you did not move, you did not breathe; it seemed as if you were dead.

I awoke. It was early in the morning. My watch had stopped, I felt completely exhausted. I was thirsty and hungry, for I had not eaten anything since the previous morning. With weariness and disgust, I pushed away the gold which but a little time before had delighted my foolish heart; now in my perplexity I was completely at a loss what to do with it. I could not leave it lying about. I tried to put it back into the purse – no, impossible. None of my windows opened onto the sea, so with immense effort I gathered it from all over the room and stored it in a large cupboard which stood in a recess. I only left a few handfuls lying about. When I had accomplished this task, I sat down exhausted in an armchair and waited until the house began to stir. Then I had breakfast brought up to me and sent for the landlord.

I told him that I intended setting up house and sought his advice on how to proceed. He recommended as personal servant a man named Bendel, whose honest and intelligent countenance immediately appealed to me. It is he who, from that day forwards, has stood by my side with deepest devotion in all my miseries and has shared with me my gloomy destiny. I spent the entire day in my room engaging servants, talking to tailors, shoemakers and tradesmen, organizing my household, purchasing large quantities of precious objects and jewels only in order to get rid of some of my stocks of gold, but it seemed as though it would never diminish.

All the time I was beset by anxious qualms. I dared not leave my room and before dusk I had forty wax candles lit so as to illuminate the room from all sides before I emerged from the dark. I thought with apprehension of the ugly scene with the schoolboys and decided, however hardly it taxed my courage, to test public opinion once more. The moon was very bright during those nights. Late one evening, I put on a large cloak and a wide-brimmed hat, which I pulled down over my eyes. Trembling like a criminal, I left the house by stealth. Having reached a remote square in the city I stepped out of the protecting shadow of the houses into the moonlight, prepared to learn my destiny from the lips of passers-by.

Spare me, dear friend, the details of the painful experiences which I had to undergo. The women mostly gave vent to expressions of pity; it was no less wounding than the derision of the young or the contempt of the men, especially of those who were fat and portly and who themselves boasted a large shadow. A beautiful young girl, who followed her parents demurely and modestly, casting her eyes down, suddenly glanced at me with a glowing look; then, startled at perceiving my predicament, hid her beautiful face behind her veil and silently went on her way. I could bear it no longer. Tears streamed down my face and with a broken heart I hurried back into the dark. I groped my way along the houses unsteadily and slowly went back to my hotel.

I could not sleep at all that night. The next morning I had but one concern: to find the man in grey. Perhaps I might be lucky enough to find him and to discover that he also regretted our foolish bargain. I sent for Bendel – he seemed a competent and capable fellow – and gave him a minute description of the man who, as I told him, had in his possession a treasure without which my life was not worth living. I told him the time and the place where I had met him, described the people who had been present, and gave him some added clues: he should enquire after a telescope, a Turkish carpet, a sumptuous tent and three black horses which were all connected in some way with the strange man to whom nobody had paid much attention and who had robbed me of my happiness and peace of mind. When I had finished I brought out as much gold as I was able to carry and added jewels and precious stones to the pile.

"Bendel," I said, "this opens many doors and makes the impossible possible. Don't be sparing with it – you know I am not; but go and bring back to me those tidings on which alone rest my hopes."

He left, and late in the evening he returned, dejected and sad. None of the servants of Mr John, not any of his guests whom he had interviewed, remembered anything about the man in the grey coat. The new telescope was there but no one knew where it had come from; so were the carpet and the tent – no one had yet removed them from the hill. The lackeys boasted of their master's riches but none of them could say when or where these things had come from. The Squire seemed to like them but did not bother about them much, and as to the horses, he had given them to the young gentlemen who had been riding them and who were delighted with his generosity. Such was Bendel's exhaustive report; I could not help praising his zeal and intelligent conduct, despite the negative result of his search. I dismissed him gloomily and asked him to leave me alone. He continued, however.

"I have," he said, "reported to my master on the matter which seemed to him the most important, but there is also a message I was asked to deliver by someone I met this morning at the door when I set out on my unsuccessful quest. Here it is, in the man's own words: 'Tell Mr Peter Schlemihl that he will not find me here any more. I have to go overseas and a favourable wind calls me to the port. But in a year and a day I shall have the honour to call on him to propose to him what I believe to be a most acceptable bargain. Convey my most respectful compliments and thanks to your master.' I asked for his name but he said you knew him well."

"What did he look like?" I exclaimed, full of forebodings. Bendel described the man in grey feature by feature, word by word, precisely as he had described him to the others when enquiring about him.

"Miserable fool!" I cried in despair, "that is the very man whom I had asked you to search for." Bendel looked like a man who had suddenly recovered his sight.

"It must have been he!" he exclaimed, "and I, silly deluded fool that I am, did not recognize him and have betrayed my trust."

He broke into a flood of bitter self-reproaches and his despair was such that I felt sorry for him. I tried to comfort him, assuring him that I did not doubt his loyalty, and then sent him off to the port to try, if possible, to trace the strange man. But that very morning many ships which had been port-bound by unfavourable winds, had put to sea to other lands and distant shores and the man in grey had vanished like a shadow, leaving no trace behind.

3

WHAT USE WOULD WINGS BE to a man bound in iron fetters? They would only drive him to even greater despair. There I was, like Fafner in his lair, out of reach of human help, starving as it were in the midst of riches. My gold gave me no joy; I cursed it, for it had cut me off from all that I treasured in life. Carrying my sinister secret in my heart, I was afraid of the meanest of my servants, whom I could not but envy, for he had his shadow and could show himself in the sun. Alone in my apartments I pined away the days and nights eating out my heart with sorrow.

My faithful servant Bendel reproached himself ceaselessly for having, as he thought, betrayed his master's confidence by failing to recognize the man he had been sent out to find and who, he understood, was responsible for my sad condition. I myself could not blame him for I recognized only too well that behind this strange event stood the uncanny figure of the man in grey. But to leave nothing untried I sent Bendel one day with a costly diamond ring to the City's most famous portrait painter to invite him to come and see me. On his arrival, I sent my servants away, locked the door behind me, and after praising the painter's work I enjoined him to strictest secrecy and broached the subject which was such a load on my mind.

"Sir," I began, "would you consent to provide a shadow for an individual who, in circumstances which are most deplorable and unfortunate, has been deprived of his own?"

"Do you mean you want me to paint a shadow for this unfortunate friend of yours?"

"Precisely that." I replied.

"May I ask by what act of clumsiness or negligence your friend has lost his shadow?"

"That is immaterial now; but if I remember rightly," I lied insolently, "during a winter journey last year in Russia it was so cold that his shadow froze to the ground so fast that he could not re-move it."

"The false shadow which I could provide in paint," the artist replied coldly, "would be of a kind which would be lost at the slightest movement, especially in the case of a man who, judging by your story, showed such feeble attachment to his own shadow. The safest and most sensible thing for a man to do who has lost his shadow, is to avoid walking in the sun." He got up, and casting a piercing glance at me which I could not meet, he left the room. Disconsolate, I sank back into my chair hiding my face in my hands.

Thus Bendel found me when he entered the room. Seeing the state I was in, he wanted to withdraw quietly and respectfully. I looked up and, unable to bear my sorrow any longer, decided to tell him about it.

"Bendel," I said, "you alone see and respect my suffering without wishing to probe into it, yet sharing it with me; come close to me now – I will take you into my confidence. As I have not withheld from you the abundance of my gold, so I shall not withhold from you the weight of my sorrow. Bendel, don't leave me. Here am I – rich, generous, kind-hearted – and you would think that the world should honour me. Yet you see me shun the world, for the world has judged me and rejected me and you, too, will reject me when you have learnt of my dreadful secret. I am rich, generous and kind but – Oh, God! I have no shadow."

"No shadow?" repeated the good fellow, as tears welled into his eyes, "and that it should be my fate to serve a gentleman who has no shadow!" He lapsed into a gloomy silence and I sat there hiding my face in my hands.

"Bendel," I resumed at last, tremblingly, "now I have told you the worst, I am in your hands and you can go and bear witness against me."

He seemed to struggle with himself but finally he threw himself at my feet and, taking my hand, bathed it with his tears.

"No," he said, "Let the world say what it likes, I will not leave my gracious master for the sake of a shadow. I will do what is right, not what seems expedient. I shall lend you my shadow and help you in any way I can; and when I cannot, at least I will share your sorrow."

I embraced him, overcome by such devotion, for I was convinced that he was not doing this for the sake of my gold. From that day on, my whole way of life changed; it is impossible for me to describe with what care and circumspection Bendel covered up my defect. He was ever in front of me or by my side, anticipating everything, providing for every contingency that might suddenly arise, and covering me with his shadow when necessary, for he was fortunately taller and broader than myself.

Thus I ventured out once again to play my part in society. Circumstances forced me to act the role of a man of whims and fancies; but these are readily accepted and, in fact, expected of a rich man. As long as my true condition remained unknown, I enjoyed all the honour and esteem that went with riches. I looked forward with tranquillity to the end of the period of one year and one day when I would receive the visit of the mysterious man in grey. I was well aware that I ought not to remain too long in this place where I had already been seen without a shadow and might therefore be betrayed; also the thought and memory of my first visit to Mr John's was somewhat depressing. I told myself that what I was doing here was merely a kind of rehearsal which would enable me later on to behave with greater sureness and self-confidence. Yet, what held me was the most powerful anchor of all: it was vanity which made me stay when I should have left.

The beautiful Fanny, whom I had met again and who did not remember having seen me before, paid some attention to me, for now I also had wit and intelligence. When I talked, people listened, and I myself could not think how I had acquired the art of easy and brilliant conversation. Having made the impression on her which I desired I, of course, became exactly what she wanted: a fool who ran after her – which I did against great odds, for I could pursue her only in the shade or in the dusk. It was my ambition to play upon her own vanity – but try as I might, my heart was not in the game.

But why go into the details of this commonplace story? You yourself have told me many like it. They followed a well-established pattern. However, in this case the well-worn comedy in which I good-humouredly played my hackneyed role, reached an unusual climax, unforeseen by actors and onlookers alike.

According to my custom, one beautiful evening I gave a party in an illuminated garden. I was walking arm-in-arm with the young lady some distance away from the rest of the party, trying hard to make polite and pleasant conversation. She was looking modestly at the ground and gently returned the pressure of my hand. Suddenly the moon broke through the clouds, throwing her shadow in front of us but not my own. She was startled and looked at me with alarm and then again at the ground, as if to search for the missing shadow. The expression on her face betrayed her thoughts. The whole spectacle was so comic that I could have burst out laughing, yet at the same time, a chill crept up my spine.

She fainted in my arms and I let her gently sink to the ground. Like an arrow from the bow I dashed past my bewildered guests, rushed through the house and reached the front door. I threw myself into the first carriage that drew up outside and drove back to the city where, to my misfortune, I had left Bendel. He was startled at my appearance. A word of explanation and post horses were ordered, I only took one of my servants with me – a crafty scoundrel appropriately called Rascal, who had managed to make himself useful to me and who could not possibly have known what had happened. We travelled thirty miles during the night. I had left Bendel behind to settle my affairs, scatter gifts and pack the most necessary things. When he joined me next day, I threw myself into his arms, I swore to be more careful in future. We continued our journey uninterrupted beyond the frontier and over a mountain range, and only when I had put such a barrier between myself and that place of misfortune, did I consent to rest awhile at a small unknown watering place to recover from the effects of my exertions.

4

I MUST NOW HURRY OVER a part of my story on which I should be delighted to dwell a little longer if I could but conjure up in my memory the spirit of that period. But the colour which gave it life and which alone could do so again has faded and if I search my heart for that intoxication which was once so powerful – the sorrows, the happiness and the heavenly delusion – I am like a man striking at a rock in search of water which is not there. The inspiration has left me for ever and how different that time appears to me now. The part I tried to play in this watering place was that of a tragic hero, but being an amateur, and with very little talent at that, I soon forgot my role and fell in love with a pair of beautiful blue eyes. The parents of the young girl, deceived by the trappings of my wealth, eagerly tried to bring the marriage about, and the vulgar farce finally ended in humiliation. That is all there is to it; it all sounds so stupid and commonplace to me now, and yet how terrible that it should, when it seemed to be so romantic and moving then. Mina! As I wept when I lost you I now weep over the fact that you mean nothing more to me. Have I become so old? O pitiful intellect of man! what would I not give for one heartbeat of those days, for one moment of that illusion. It cannot be. I am like a solitary wave on a vast sea, unable to recall even the memory of what I felt at the time.

I had sent Bendel ahead of me with bags of gold to furnish and equip a suitable house for me in the town. He had spent a great deal of money and talked mysteriously of the illustrious stranger whom he was serving, who did not wish to be named. This gave the citizens all sorts of ideas. As soon as the house was ready we started out on our journey. Bendel had returned to collect me and travelled with me now.

About an hour's distance from the little town we found our way barred by a festive crowd. The coach stopped, we heard music, the ringing of bells and a salute of guns, and in the crowd people were cheering. A group of young maidens clad in white, came up to the door of my carriage. All were outstandingly beautiful, but one among them outshone them all as the sun outshines the brightest stars. She stepped forwards out of the group, modestly curtsied before me and presented to me on a silken cushion a wreath of laurels, olive branches and roses, murmuring as she did so something about majesty, respect and love. The meaning of this address of welcome escaped me but the silvery tone of her voice was enchanting. She seemed like a dream from heaven. After the address a choir of young girls intoned a hymn praising the good king and the happiness of his people.

All this, my dear friend, took place in the bright midday sun. She was standing two paces away from the open carriage door but I, shadowless, dared not brave the sunlight to fall on my knees before her as I would have liked. What would I not have given for a shadow at that moment. There I was, unable to move, hiding my fear and perplexity in the dark recesses of the coach. At last Bendel put an end to my embarrassment; he jumped down from the other side of the carriage and I handed him a small casket containing a gorgeous diamond tiara, which had been destined to adorn the head of the beautiful Fanny. He stepped forwards and spoke on my behalf. His master, he said, could not accept this honour – there must have been some error – but wished to convey his grateful thanks to the citizens for this demonstration of goodwill. With these words he lifted the wreath from the cushion and put the tiara in its place; then with a reverend gesture, he bade the young girl to rise, and made the assembled magistrates, clergy and other dignitaries understand that the reception had come to an end. He ordered the crowds to make room for the carriage, jumped into it and off we went at a gallop, not stopping until we reached the city, where we had to pass through a triumphal arch of branches and flowers. All the while, guns were booming in salute.

The carriage drew up at my house and, springing nimbly out, I escaped through the door from another crowd which had assembled to greet me. There was loud cheering under my windows when I was inside. I ordered double ducats to be scattered among the crowd.

At night the town was illuminated. I was still unable to make out what all this could mean and whom I was being mistaken for. I sent out my servant Rascal to obtain information. He gathered that there had been a rumour that the King of Prussia was travelling through the district under the title of Count and that the citizens, having made preparations to receive him, had recognized my aide-de-camp, who in turn had betrayed his and my true identity; the joy of knowing their King to be in their midst was great indeed. It had not at first been realized that I wished to preserve the strictest incognito and that it was therefore unseemly to try to intrude upon my privacy. It had been greatly appreciated that I had expressed my displeasure with such graciousness and it was fervently hoped that I would forgive the excess of zeal which the citizens had shown in their great loyalty.

The whole thing had seemed such a joke to my scoundrel of a servant, that he had done everything he could to confirm the good people in this belief. He gave me a most entertaining report of what had happened and, seeing that it greatly amused me, he boasted about the mischief he had done. Shall I confess? I was greatly flattered to have been – even for a moment – taken for the King. I organized a garden fête in front of the house for the following evening, to which I issued invitations to practically the whole town. It is astounding how the mysterious power of my gold, Bendel's efforts and Rascal's inventiveness succeeded; and how it was possible to organize everything in such a short space of time. The pomp and luxury displayed and the ingenuity of the illuminations, were such that I felt completely at ease. I could not find fault with anything and only praised the diligence of my servants.

Evening and darkness came, and with it the first guests arrived and were introduced to me. As if by general consent, the title Majesty was never used; instead I often heard, uttered in deep humility, "The Count." What was I to do? I accepted it and from that moment I was "Count Peter." But in the midst of this festive crowd my heart was longing only for her. She arrived late – the crown of the evening – wearing the crown I had given her the day before. She modestly walked behind her parents, quite unconscious of her beauty. The game warden, his wife and Mina their daughter were introduced to me. I knew how to flatter and to say all sorts of pleasant things to the parents but I stood before their daughter like a schoolboy, unable to utter a single word. I finally managed to say that I was greatly honoured by her presence and invited her to preside over the festivities. Blushingly and with touching simplicity, she declined the honour but I, more abashed before her than she before me, offered her my humble respects in the presence of all the guests who, taking the cue from their host, gladly followed suit. It was a beautiful and festive evening presided over by innocence, grace and dignity. Mina's happy parents believed that it was out of respect for them that I had honoured their child. I myself was in the seventh heaven. I had all the jewels brought – pearls, precious stones – which I had previously purchased to get rid of some of the cumbersome gold – and had them put onto two covered plates on the table. In the name of the "Queen of the evening" they were taken round among the guests for each of the ladies to select what she fancied most. Meanwhile, gold was being freely distributed among the cheering crowds outside.

The next morning Bendel confided to me that his suspicions about Rascal's dishonesty had been confirmed. He had embezzled several sacks of gold.

"Don't let us envy," I said, "the poor devil his trifling loot. It's a pleasure to me to give to everyone, so why not to him? He served me well yesterday, like all my other servants who have helped me to arrange this delightful party."

The incident was mentioned no more; Rascal remained my head servant, Bendel my friend and confidant. The latter imagined my wealth to be inexhaustible and never inquired where it came from. He seemed to have understood my intentions and did his best to invent opportunities for me to display and to squander it. Of that unknown, pale, sneaking fellow he only knew that it was in his power to lift the curse which weighed on me and that I was afraid of the man on whom all my hopes were fixed. Besides, he thought that I was convinced that the stranger could find me anywhere, whereas I could never find him and that I had therefore abandoned my search and was waiting for the promised day. The magnificence of my party and my generosity at first confirmed the credulous citizens in their preconceived opinion as to my identity. Soon, however, it became known from the newspapers that the fabulous journey of the King of Prussia had merely been an unfounded rumour. But once a king, I had to remain a king and one of the richest and most kingly at that. But what king, no one quite knew. The world has never had cause to complain of any scarcity of monarchs, especially nowadays. And so the good people, who had never before seen one with their own eyes, happily guessed and changed their guesses from day to day. Count Peter, however, continued to be my name.

One day there arrived among the visitors to the Spa, a business man who had become rich by fraudulent bankruptcy, and who enjoyed general esteem. He cast a wide, though somewhat pale, shadow. He was determined to display his wealth and even to compete with me. I called upon my purse and soon I had got the poor devil into such straits that in order to save his reputation he had to go bankrupt once more and cross the mountains into another country.

53

Thus I was rid of him and I must confess that I am responsible for having made many a loafer and vagabond in the district.

Despite the kingly pomp and luxury with which I held sway over my world, I lived a quiet and retiring life. I made a point of acting with the greatest caution in all things; for instance, under no pretext whatsoever was anyone except Bendel allowed to see me in my own rooms. Whenever the sun shone I remained cloistered there with him alone.

"The Count is engaged in his study," the people said; and the messengers who came and went (dispatched by me on the most trivial business) bore out the impression that I was engaged on some important work.

Only in the evening I received company, protected by the deep shade of the trees; or in my salon, whose magnificent lighting had been skilfully arranged by Bendel so that no shadows fell. Whenever I went out – always under Bendel's watchful eye – my one goal was the game warden's garden. His daughter had become the one object of my existence; the core of my life was my love for her.

My dear Chamisso, I hope you have not completely forgotten what love is like, for I must leave a great deal to your imagining. Mina was truly lovely and lovable, a good and gentle child. I had captured her imagination entirely. In her modesty she wondered why I should have stooped to her. But she returned love for love with all the ardour of innocence and youth. She loved like a woman; self-sacrificing, self-effacing, living only in him to whom she had given herself; careless of her own fate: in a word, she truly loved.

But oh, those terrible yet unforgettable hours! How often I poured myself out to Bendel as I came to my senses after the first unthinking transports of rapture. How bitterly I blamed myself that I, a shadowless being, should have corrupted this angelic girl, with lies and cunning stealing her pure love. Sometimes I determined to tell her all; sometimes I swore to tear myself away from her and escape; then again I weakened and begged Bendel to arrange for me to visit her in the game warden's garden that evening.

Sometimes I buoyed myself up with hopes of the imminent visit of the mysterious man in grey, then again I was cast into despair when I thought that he might not come. I had worked out the day when I might expect to see him. He had said he would come in a year and a day and I relied on his word.

The parents were worthy, good old folk, loving their only child most dearly. My continued pursuit of Mina and our mutual attachment had taken them by surprise and they did not know how to cope with the situation. It had never occurred to them that Count Peter would so much as look at their child; and now it was clear that he actually loved her and was loved in return. The mother, no doubt, was vain enough to dream of the possibility of such a marriage and even to try to bring it about; but the sound common sense of the old man refused to entertain such fantasies. They believed in the honesty of my love and could do nothing but pray for their daughter.

In my hand at this moment is a letter which I received from Mina in those days. Here it is in her own hand.

I know I am a weak and foolish girl, believing that my lover will never hurt me because I love him so much.

Oh, you are so kind, so unspeakably good to me; but don't misunderstand me, please. Make no sacrifices for me – do not think of it even. I would hate myself if you did. You have made me happy beyond words, you have taught me to love you. But leave me now; it is not in my stars that I should have you. Count Peter is not mine but belongs to the great world. With what pride I shall hear: 'This was he – that he has done – there he has been loved and adored.' When I think of this, I could blame you for forgetting your high calling for the sake of a simple girl. Leave me, if you don't want to make me unhappy – I, who have been so happy because of you. Have I not entwined myself in your life like the olive branch and the rosebud in the garland which I was so proud to give you? I hold you in my heart, my beloved, do not be afraid to leave me. And if I die I shall have been so unspeakably blissful through you.

You can imagine how these words pierced my heart. I told her that I was not what I appeared to be; that I was merely a rich but infinitely wretched man. There was, I told her, a curse upon me, which should be the only secret between us for I still hoped that I would be delivered from it. The whole bane of my existence was this: that I might drag her – the light and soul and happiness of my life – into the abyss with me. She wept to see me so unhappy. She was so tender, so devoted. How glad she would have been to sacrifice herself to save me a single tear.

But she was very far from guessing what I meant. She probably believed I was a prince condemned to banishment, a noble leader unjustly disgraced, around whom her loving imagination painted a thousand heroic situations.

"Mina," I said to her one day, "on the last day of next month, my fate may change and be decided; if that does not happen I must die, for I cannot bear to make you unhappy."

She hid her face on my shoulders. "If your fate changes, all I want to know is that you are happy, for I have no claim on you. But if you become more miserable, then only let me stay with you to help you bear it."

"Dearest, take back those rash and foolish promises. Can you guess at my curse and my misery? Your lover – do you know what he is? You see me trembling at the thought that you might discover my horrible secret."

She fell sobbing at my feet and renewed her declaration with a solemn vow.

The game warden now entered and I announced to him my determination formally to ask for the hand of his daughter on the first day of the coming month, I fixed that date, I told him, because in the meantime things might happen which would greatly influence my fortunes. What could never change was my love for his daughter.

The good old man started back in amazement as these words burst from my lips. He embraced me, then dropped his arms in confusion at having forgotten himself so far. He stopped to think, doubts sprang up in his mind; he began tentatively to speak of a dowry and the future security of his beloved daughter. I told him I was glad he had brought this to my mind.

"I want to settle here," I said, "and lead a carefree life in this neighbourhood where I appear to be well-liked."

I told him to buy, in his daughter's name, the finest estates he could find on the market, referring to me for payment. No one, surely, could serve me better in this matter than the father of my sweetheart. This gave him a good deal of trouble, for there was some stranger in the same market who always seemed to forestall him and he only made purchases in the amount of about 1,000,000 florins.

I confess this was a sort of innocent trick to get rid of him, to which I had been reduced once before, for it must be admitted the old man was rather a bore. His wife, on the other hand, was somewhat deaf and unlike him, not always jealous of the honour of entertaining the noble Count.

The old lady now joined us and the happy parents begged me to spend the evening with them. But I dared not stay a moment longer. Already the moon was rising and my time was up.

The next evening I returned to the game warden's garden. I had wrapped myself in a dark cloak and my hat was slouched over my eyes. I walked towards Mina: as she raised her eyes and looked at me, I thought I saw her shudder. The terrible night in which I had been seen shadowless in the moonlight returned vividly to my mind. It was Mina, right enough; but did she, too, have an inkling of what I really was? She remained thoughtful and silent as we sat together. My heart was heavy. I rose to go. She threw herself speechless into my arms. I left her.

But now I often found her in tears; my own soul grew more and more oppressed; only the old people were blissfully happy. The fatal day drew nearer, heavy and ominous like a thundercloud. When at last the eve arrived, I could hardly breathe. I had taken the precaution of filling some chests with gold. I sat up waiting for midnight. It struck.

All day I sat, my eyes riveted to the hands of the clock. The minutes, as they ticked past, smote me like the blows of a dagger. At every sound I sprang to my feet. Day dawned. The leaden hours crowded one on another; it was morning – then evening, night. The hands of the clock moved slowly on and hope was dying. Eleven struck and no one appeared. The last minutes of the last hour slipped away and still no one. The first stroke and then the last stroke of twelve sounded. I sank on my bed in an agony of despair. Tomorrow – shadowless for ever – I must ask for the hand of my love. Towards morning I fell into a heavy sleep.

5

I T WAS STILL EARLY when I was woken by voices in my antechamber raised in furious dispute. I listened: Bendel was refusing entry to my room. Rascal swore loudly that he would take no orders from a fellow servant and dared him to stop him if he could. The kindly Bendel warned that such language, if it reached my ears, might easily lose him a good place; but Rascal threatened to lay violent hands upon him if he impeded his entrance any longer.

I was already half-dressed and now flung the door open angrily.

"What do you want, scoundrel?" I called out to Rascal.

He drew back a couple of steps.

"May it please your lordship," he said, with cool effrontery, "to show me for once your shadow; it is such a beautiful, sunny day outside."

I felt as if I had been struck by lightning and for a long time was unable to speak.

"How dare a servant presume such a thing of his master—" I began.

"A servant may be an honest man," he said with irritating calmness, "and yet refuse to serve a shadowless master – I demand my discharge."

I tried another tactic. "My dear Rascal," I said, "Who has put this disastrous idea into your head? How can you imagine—"

"People say," he continued in the same tone, "that you have no shadow; in short, either show me your shadow or let me go."

Bendel, pale and trembling but more in control of himself than I, made me a quick sign to seek refuge in the usual price of silence – a heavy bribe. Rascal flung the gold at my feet.

"I will take nothing," he cried, "from a shadowless man." He turned his back on me, put his hat on his head and strode slowly out of the room, whistling a tune. I stood as if turned to stone, watching him go, my mind empty and numb.

Heavy and melancholy and with death in my heart,

I prepared to keep my promise and, less like a suitor than a criminal before his judges, to show myself in the game warden's garden. I drove to the shady arbour which had been called after me, where as usual we had arranged to meet. Mina's mother came forwards to greet me, gay and carefree. Mina was sitting there, pale and lovely like the first snow of autumn that falls on summer's last flower, soon to dissolve into bitter drops. The game warden, holding a letter in his hand, was pacing up and down in a state of violent agitation which, as the colour came and went in his cheeks, he tried in vain to conceal. He came towards me as I entered and in an unsteady voice asked to speak to me alone. The path where he wanted me to follow him led to an open, sunny part of the garden. I sat down without a word. There was a long silence which even the good mother dared not break.

The game warden continued to pace up and down the arbour. Finally he stood before me, glanced at the paper in his hand and fixed me with a penetrating look.

"Count Peter," he said, "Have you never heard of one Peter Schlemihl?" I was speechless. "A man," he continued, "of excellent character and great accomplishments." He waited for my answer.

"Supposing I told you I were he?"

"A man," he cried violently, "who has somehow lost his shadow."

"Oh," cried Mina, "my fears had told me. I knew long ago that he had no shadow." She threw herself into the arms of her mother who, holding her close, tenderly reproached her for having kept such a fatal suspicion from her. But she, poor girl, like Arethusa, was dissolved into a fountain of tears, which flowed abundantly at the sound of my voice and at my approach tempestuously burst forth.

"And so," cried the game warden furiously, "with incredible impudence you tried to deceive us – and you pretended to love her! – that poor girl whom you have so tricked and humiliated. Look at her now – her tears and the misery to which you have reduced her. What a terrible thing to have done!"

I was so completely overcome that I hardly knew what I said.

"After all," I muttered, "it's only a matter of a shadow – nothing but a shadow and surely one can do without that? No need to make such a fuss about it." But even as I spoke the words seemed so meaningless that I stopped. He did not deign to answer and I managed to add: "What a man has lost today, he may find again tomorrow."

"Tell me one thing," he said angrily, "just explain how you came to lose your shadow."

"Some boorish rascal" – I was driven again to clumsy lying – "trod so rudely on my shadow that he tore a great hole in it. I sent it to be mended – money can do most things, you know. I should have got it back yesterday."

"Very well, sir, very well," he replied. "You want to marry my daughter – others do, too. As her father I must take care of her interest. I give you three days which you may spend in getting hold of a shadow. If in that time you show up with a properly fitting shadow, you will be welcome; but if not, on the fourth day, I may as well tell you, my daughter shall be married to someone else."

I tried to get a word with Mina but, drenched in tears, she clung closer to her mother who, with a silent gesture, bid me to go. I slunk away as if the gates of life had closed behind me.

Throwing off Bendel's kindly guardianship, I wandered aimlessly in my distraction through the fields and woods. Sweat poured down my face, wild cries broke from my lips. I was nearly insane.

I don't know how long I wandered in this state when suddenly, in a sunny meadow, I felt someone's hand on my sleeve. I stopped and looked round – and there stood the man in the grey coat. He seemed to have been running after me, for he was out of breath.

"I had an appointment with you today," he began immediately. "You seem not to have been able to wait for me; but no harm is done yet – you will take my advice: redeem your shadow again; I have it here waiting for you, and then go back at once. The game warden will receive you with open arms. The whole business was just a joke. Rascal, who has betrayed you and who is courting your sweetheart, I will take care of – he's ripe for it."

I stood there as in a dream.

"Due today?" I reckoned the time over again; he was right. I had been a day out in my calculations. I put my hand on the bag in my breast pocket; he guessed my meaning and drew back a step or two.

"No, no, sir," he said, "you keep that," I stared at him questioningly as he went on: "I just ask for one little thing as a memento. Please be good enough to sign this note." On the scrap of parchment which he held out I read the following words:

"I hereby undertake to deliver over my soul to the bearer after its natural separation from my body; in witness whereof my signature is affixed."

I looked with dumb amazement from the piece of writing to the unknown man in grey. In the meantime, he dipped a newly cut quill in a drop of my blood, which was flowing from a scratch made by a thorn in my hand. He handed the quill to me.

"But who are you?" I brought out at last.

"Never you mind," he answered. "Can't you see I'm a poor devil; a kind of scientist or physician, you might say, who gets small thanks for the great favours he confers on his friends; and whose sole pleasure on earth is to experiment a little. But please, just sign your name – there at the bottom, on the right. Peter Schlemihl."

I shook my head. "I'm sorry, sir. I will not sign."

"What!" he cried, with seeming surprise. "Why ever not?"

"It seems to me rather a weighty matter to give my soul in exchange for my shadow."

"Weighty!" he repeated after me and burst out laughing. "And what, may I ask, do you imagine your soul is? Have you ever seen it? And what do you intend doing with it once you are dead? Thank your stars that you have found a collector sufficiently interested to wish to buy, even during your lifetime, the reversion of this quantity X, this galvanic force, this polarized potential, or whatever we may like to call this illusive something; and to be willing to pay for it with something really tangible – your very own shadow, which will give you the hand of your sweetheart and the fulfilment of everything you want. Or would you rather hand over the innocent young girl to that despicable schemer, Mr Rascal? Come and see for yourself. I'll lend you the cap of invisibility" (he drew something out of his pocket) "and we'll make a little pilgrimage unseen to the game warden's garden."

I admit I hated to be made fun of by this fellow. I loathed him from the bottom of my heart; and I believe that, more than principles and prejudices, this violent personal antipathy prevented me from giving him my signature for my shadow, desperately as I needed it. The thought of going to the game warden's garden in such company was almost unbearable. That this sneaking scoundrel, this scornful, irritating imp, should put himself between me and my darling in the hour of our distress, revolted my deepest feelings. I looked on what had passed as fate and regarded my misery as inevitable. I turned upon the man and said:

"Sir, I sold you my shadow for this admittedly priceless bag. I have been sorry enough for it; if the bargain can be undone, in God's name, let us undo it."

His face darkened and he shook his head.

"I have nothing more I will sell you," I went on, "even though you offer my shadow as the price. Nor will I put my name to anything. One cannot help thinking that the little jaunt you are proposing to me would be more entertaining for you than for me. I'm sorry, but that's all there is to it. Let us go our own ways."

"I'm sorry, Mr Schlemihl," he said, "that you so lightly turn down the favours that out of the goodness of my heart I'm trying to do you; but another time I may have better luck. Goodbye till we meet again! By the by, allow me to show you that I do not let my purchases fall into disrepair; on the contrary, I know how to appreciate and take care of them."

With these words, he drew my shadow out of his pocket and, with a dexterous fling, unrolled and spread it out on the heath on the sunny side of his feet, so that he stood between the two attendant shadows, mine and his. He took a few steps to show me; my shadow seemed to belong to him as much as his own faithfully following him and conforming to all his movements.

At the sight of my poor shadow, from which I had been parted so long and which was being put to such use at the very moment when its owner was in such a bitter predicament for its sake, I felt as if my heart would break and tears started to my eyes. The loathsome wretch paraded up and down with his spoil and insolently renewed his proposals.

"You can have it still," he said, "for the stroke of a pen. One stroke that will also rescue the poor, unfortunate Mina from the arms of that scoundrel and restore her to your lordship's honourable embrace." Overcome by anger and misery, I could not speak; I turned away and motioned to him to go.

Meanwhile, Bendel had been anxiously looking for me and now appeared on the scene. The good soul, seeing my distress and noticing my shadow, which he could hardly mistake, bound to the figure of the strange man in grey, immediately set about trying to restore my property to me by force. Not being able to get a firm hold on something so frail and elusive, he ordered the man in a peremptory tone, to abandon what did not belong to him. This latter, in reply merely turned his back on the well-meaning fellow and walked away. Bendel followed him closely and, lifting up the stout blackthorn cudgel which he carried, commanded the man to give up my shadow, reinforcing his argument with a shower of pitiless blows. The man in grey, accustomed no doubt to this kind of treatment, merely bent his head, arched his shoulders and continued silently on his way, taking

with him my shadow and my faithful man. For a
long time the dull thud of blows echoed over the
heath. It faded at last in the distance. I was alone
with my misery once more.

6

ALONE ON THE DREARY HEATH, I gave vent to my misery, which seemed to relieve me a little from the burden of my intolerable grief. But I could see no bounds, no end and no way out of my overwhelming anguish. I dwelt with a kind of wild fascination on the iniquitous suggestions with which the mysterious grey man had rubbed salt into my wounds. I remembered Mina, and her tender and lovely figure rose before me, pale and tearful as I had seen her last in the hour of my cruel humiliation; then the sinister shade of Rascal seemed to rise mockingly between us. I covered my face, I fled across the heath but the ghastly vision still pursued me. I sank at last breathless to the ground with tears of exhaustion and despair.

And all this for the sake of a shadow! A shadow which the stroke of a pen would have given back to me! I brooded again on the strange deal which had been proposed to me. I had neither argument nor reason left to support my refusal.

The day wore on. I stilled my hunger with wild berries and my thirst from the nearest stream. Night fell. I lay down under a tree. The dew woke me next morning from a restless sleep, broken by my own bitter moaning. Bendel must have lost track of me and I was glad of it. I had no desire to return to the haunts of man; I shunned them, feeling like a wild beast of the mountains. For three anxious days I lived like this.

On the morning of the fourth day I found myself on a sandy plain, where the sun was shining brightly. I sat down on an outcrop of rock in the sunshine, rejoicing for a while in its long forbidden warmth. My heart still fed on its own despair. Suddenly I was disturbed by a gentle rustling. I looked round in alarm, ready to escape – no one was in sight. But on the sunny sand beside me a human shadow passed, not unlike my own and apparently straying about without an owner.

A mighty urge rose within me. Shadow, I thought, are you seeking a master? I will be your master. And

I sprang forwards to seize it. I imagined that if I could only step on the shadow so that its feet met mine it would attach itself to me and in time grow used to my company.

As I moved forwards the shadow fled and I was forced to give chase to the light-footed fugitive. The longing to be delivered from my predicament lent me unaccustomed speed. The shadow made for a distant wood, in the darkness of which I would have lost it at once. Spurred by this fear I redoubled my efforts and began to gain on the shadow. I came closer and closer – now it was within reach. Suddenly it stopped and turned to face me. Like a lion on his prey, I sprang upon it with a mighty effort to hold it fast. To my amazement, I found I had thrown myself against something which offered a powerful physical resistance; from an unseen hand I received the most violent blows imaginable. The sudden shock of fear made me struggle desperately to hold down the invisible opponent. I plunged forwards and fell to the ground; beneath me on his back was a man whom I held fast, who now was visible.

The whole affair now could be easily explained. The man must have been holding the magic bird's nest which makes its owner – though not that owner's shadow – invisible, and under the impact of my attack had thrown it away. I looked round and immediately saw the shadow of the invisible bird's nest. I sprang up and seized this shadow and, in so doing, found myself, unseen as well as shadowless, with the charm itself in my hand.

The man rose quickly. He looked anxiously for his successful assailant but could not see either him or his shadow on the broad, sunny plain. The absence of the shadow seemed to alarm him most for he had had no time to observe nor reason to suspect that I was the shadowless man.

As soon as he realized that every trace of me and the magic bird's nest had completely vanished, he threw up his hands and began to tear his hair in desperation. But as for me, the treasure which I had stolen gave me the means and the desire to mingle with my kind once more. It was not hard to find an excuse for this despicable theft: indeed, it seemed to me that no excuse was needed. To escape any possible pangs of conscience, I hurried away without even looking back at my wretched victim, whose miserable cries followed after me. This, at least, is how I saw it at the time.

I longed to return to the game warden's garden, to see for myself whether, what the man in grey had told me, was true. I had no idea, however, where I was and in order to get my bearings, I climbed the nearest hill, from the top of which I saw the little town and the game warden's house and garden spread out at my feet. My heart pounded with excitement and my eyes were wet with tears of joy. I was going to see her again! Eager longing sped my anxious footsteps down the shortest path. I passed a crowd of peasants leaving the town. They talked of me and Rascal and the game warden. I did not stop to listen; I hurried on.

I entered the garden, full of trepidation. I thought I heard a laugh beside me; with a start I looked round but could see nothing. I walked on and human footsteps seemed to be pacing beside me. Still nothing in sight – I thought my ears had deceived me. It was early, no one was in the arbour, the garden was empty. I wandered through the familiar paths until I came to the house. The same sound followed me – more distinctly this time. I sat dejectedly on a seat in the sunshine, immediately opposite the front door. I seemed to hear my invisible tormentor laugh insultingly as he sat down beside me.

Suddenly the front door opened and out walked the game warden with some papers in his hand. There seemed to be a greyish mist before my eyes – I turned my head and there – to my horror – beside me sat the man in grey, with a devilish smile on his lips. He had pulled his cap of invisibility over my head. At his feet my shadow lay peacefully against his and he was toying carelessly with the well-known scrap of parchment in his hand. While the game warden paced up and down in the shade of the arbour, he bent his head and whispered in my ear:

"So! At last you have accepted my offer and here we sit, two heads under one cap. Well, well! And now you may as well give me my bird's nest back again – you do not need it any more and are too honest a man to keep what does not belong to you. No, no, don't mention it – it was a pleasure to lend it to you, you may be sure." He took the charm from me and put it in his pocket with a laugh so loud that the game warden looked round, attracted by the noise. I sat there as if turned to stone.

"You must admit," he went on, "that such a cap is infinitely more convenient. It covers both the man and his shadow and as many others as he likes to bring to the party. Today, for instance, there are two of us." He laughed again. "Remember, Schlemihl, what is not done with a good grace at first, you may always be forced to do in the end. I think you may still pay my price for your shadow. There's still time: take back your bride and send Rascal to swing on the gallows where he belongs. Listen, I'll throw the cap into the bargain."

The mother had now joined her husband.

"What is Mina doing?" he said.

"In tears again."

"The silly girl! But there's nothing to be done about it."

"True. But to marry her off to another so soon! O my dear husband, you are being cruel to your own child."

"Wife, you don't see clearly. Even before she has dried her tears, when she finds herself married to a rich and respected husband, she will wake from her dream and be consoled for her disappointment. She'll live to thank us – just you wait and see."

"Please God she does!" the old woman murmured, "She already had a pretty handsome dowry but I suppose after all the scandal over that wretched adventurer, such a brilliant match as this Mr Rascal won't easily be found. Do you know just what he's worth?"

"He has 6,000,000 florins worth of landed property in this country, paid for in cash. I have the deeds here in my hand. It was he who always forestalled me when I was in the market for Mina. Besides this, he holds bills of exchange on Mr Thomas John, in excess of 3,500,000 florins."

"He must have been pilfering at a pretty rate!"

"Not at all! He has husbanded his resources while some people threw their money about."

"But a man who has been a servant!"

"Who cares? At least he has an impeccable shadow."

"Yes, but..."

The man in the grey coat laughed mockingly in my face. The door opened and Mina came out. She was leaning on her maid's arm and the silent tears poured down her lovely face. She sat down on a chair which had been brought for her under the lime trees and her father seated himself beside her. He seized her hand, at which her tears flowed more bitterly than ever.

"My dearest child," he said in the gentlest tone, "you are my good girl; try to be sensible too. You wouldn't want to grieve your old father, who is only thinking of your happiness. I quite understand, little girl, that this has been a hard knock for you. You have had the narrowest escape. Before the wicked fraud was unmasked you loved the unworthy fellow most dearly. I know, Mina, and I don't blame you a bit. I loved him, too, when I thought he was rich and noble. But you see what it has come to. Even a poodle has a shadow and could I let my precious, my only daughter be married to such a man? Never! You must put him out of your head. Listen, my Mina: a suitor is asking for you – a respectable man who does not fear the sun; no count, indeed, but owner of ten millions – ten times more than you have ever owned. A man, too, who can make my dear child happy. So do not oppose me. Say nothing – be my good, obedient daughter. Trust your loving father and let him take care of you. Dry your tears now and say you will marry Mr Rascal. Come now, will you promise?"

Her answer was almost inaudible. "There's nothing in the world I want any more." she said. "I will do as my father tells me."

At this Mr Rascal was announced and insolently joined the party. Mina sank fainting to the ground. My evil genius fixed me with an angry look.

"Can you bear *that* too?" he whispered. "What runs in your veins instead of blood?" With a swift movement he scratched my hand and the blood flowed. "So it's blood after all!" he cried scornfully. "Sign!" The parchment and the quill were in my hand.

7

I SHALL LAY MYSELF OPEN to your criticism, dear
Chamisso, which I do not try to avoid. No one
could blame me more harshly than I do myself, for
bitter remorse has long eaten up my heart. I shall
never forget that terrible moment and still look back
on it askance with deepest humiliation. Believe me,
my friend, he who carelessly steps off the straight and
narrow path, soon finds himself impelled step by step
down a very different road, along which he will be
led further and further astray. For him in vain the
Pole Star shines in heaven; there is no choice for him;
he can only descend the steep path which leads to his
inevitable fate. After the false and ill-considered step
which had brought the curse upon me, my love had
involved me in the fate of another being. What else
could I do – where I had sown perdition and salva-
tion was urgently needed – but rush forwards to save,

at whatever cost to myself? Do not think so ill of me, Chamisso, as to imagine that I thought any price too high. No! But my soul was filled with unconquerable loathing for this mysterious intriguer and his crooked ways. Maybe I did him an injustice, but the thought of having anything further to do with him revolted me utterly. But here, as so often in my life as well as in the history of the world, the unexpected intervened. Later, I became reconciled with myself. I learnt, in the first place, to respect the inevitable and, looking back, what could be more inevitable – more so even than one's own actions – than what appeared at the time to be an accident. Next I had to learn to bow to this inevitability, as the working of Providence, which sets the machinery of the world in action, and with which we can only co-operate by moving and setting other wheels in motion. What has to be, will happen: what had to be, came to pass; and not without the intervention of that Providence, which I at last perceived as working in my fate and in that other fate so closely linked with mine.

I do not know whether it was emotional strain or physical exhaustion after the privations of the last three days; or violent agitation induced by the presence of the grey monster: but the fact is, that while preparing to sign, I fell into a deep swoon and lay for a long time as if dead.

As I came to my senses, the first sound that reached my ears was curses and the stamping of feet. I opened my eyes; it was dark. My hated companion was supporting me.

"If that isn't behaving like a silly old woman!" he scolded. "Get up like a man and finish the business as you intended. Or perhaps you still have second thoughts and want to whine a little longer." With difficulty I raised myself from the ground and looked around me. It was late evening. Festive music came from the brightly-lit house of the game warden and guests were moving in scattered groups along the garden paths. A party drew near and sat down on a seat. I could overhear their conversation. They talked of the wedding of the daughter of the house and the rich Mr Rascal, which had taken place that morning. Everything was over for me.

I tore from my head the cap of invisibility and fled in silence to hide myself in the deepest darkness of the wood, making for the garden gate by Count Peter's arbour. But my evil genius followed me unseen.

"This, then," he cried bitterly, "is my reward for taking care of the over-sensitive gentleman all day long. And so you think you can fool me after all! Very well, Mr Wronghead. Run away, but make no mistake about it, we are inseparable. You have my gold and I have your shadow. Neither of us can have any rest. Did you ever hear of a shadow abandoning its master? Yours drives me to follow you until you are ready to take it again and I get rid of it. What you have failed to do cheerfully and willingly you will be forced to do from sheer weariness in the end; man cannot escape his fate."

He pursued me with more talk in the same vein. I tried to escape but he was with me still, talking sneeringly of my shadow and his gold. My mind was in a whirl.

Through the deserted street, I hurried home. When at last I stood before my house, I could hardly recognize it. The doors were barred and behind the broken windows I could see no light. No servants seemed to be about. But my grey companion was still behind me.

"Ha, ha!" he laughed, "but you can be sure Bendel
is in. He was sent home so thoroughly worn out that
I'm sure he won't come out again yet awhile." He
laughed again. "He'll have some funny stories to
tell you. Good night for now, I'll see you again very
soon."

After I had rung several times, a light appeared
and Bendel's voice called from within: "Who's
there?" When the good fellow heard my voice he
could hardly contain himself for joy. The door was
flung open and with tears we fell into each other's
arms. I found him greatly altered – weak and ill. I
had changed too; my hair was streaked with grey.

He led me through the empty rooms to an inner
apartment which was still furnished. He brought
some food and drink and we sat down together. He
told me that on that fatal day when he had left me
in a vain attempt to recapture my shadow, he had
beaten the strange man in grey with his stick so hard
and so long, that he lost all track of me and at last
fell exhausted to the ground. Later, not being able
to find me, he had returned home and found that
the mob, incited by Rascal, had attacked the house,

breaking the windows and giving way to wanton destruction. Thus they had repaid their benefactor. My servants fled in a body. The police had banished me from the town as a suspect and given me twenty-four hours in which to leave. He had a great deal to add to what I knew already of Rascal's marriage and wealth. The scoundrel, who had instigated all these proceedings against me, must have known my secret from the beginning. It seems that, attracted by my wealth, he had forced himself upon me and that very early on he had procured a key for my safe, on the contents of which he had laid the foundation of his fortune, which he could now sit back and enjoy.

Bendel's recitation was punctuated with laments, alternating with tears of relief at seeing me again, after his desperate anxiety on my behalf, bearing my adversity with such calmness and fortitude. For this was indeed the form my despair took. My misery loomed over me, gigantic and irrevocable. I had no more tears to shed, no voice left to bemoan my misery. Coldly and indifferently, I bared my head to the storm.

"Bendel," I said, "you know my fate. This heavy penalty is not wholly undeserved. But you, an innocent man, must no longer join your fortune to mine. I will leave this very night. Saddle my horse – I shall ride alone. I command you to stay here. There must be a few boxes of gold left. I give them to you. I shall wander restlessly through the world; but if a happier day should dawn and fortune smile on me again, I will remember you. For you have been my faithful companion in many an hour of wretchedness."

Broken-hearted, the honest fellow obeyed my last command. It tore his soul but I was deaf to his protests and entreaties. He brought my horse. For the last time, I embraced him and, springing into the saddle, pursued my way from the grave of all my hopes under the cloak of night and careless whither I went. I had no goal, no wish, no hope on earth.

8

Before long, I was joined by a man who, after walking for some time by my horse's side, asked me, as we were going in the same direction, if he might throw the cloak which he carried over my crupper. I allowed him to do so without demur. He thanked me politely for this trifling favour, praised my horse and began to talk flatteringly about the happiness and influence of riches. For some time he dilated on this in a kind of soliloquy, for I did not trouble to answer.

He held forth on his views of life and the world, and soon the subject of metaphysics was introduced. From this, he held, the word was to emanate which would solve all mysteries. He developed his theme and drew his conclusions with great clarity and distinction.

You know quite well that since I struggled through the school of philosophy, I have often confessed that I do not consider myself apt for philosophical speculations and have altogether renounced this branch of learning. Since then I have allowed many questions to settle themselves as best they could and turned my back on many things which I might have mastered. Rather, I followed your advice, Chamisso, and taking common sense as my guide, as far as possible have pursued my own way. My philosopher seemed to me to build up a solid thesis with considerable skill – a thesis which seemed to be based on sound foundations and therefore stood, as it were, by its own inner necessity. But I looked in vain in the argument for the explanation I sought and hence it was to me no more than a work of art, whose completeness and graceful proportions delight the eye. I listened willingly to my eloquent companion, who distracted my attention from my own sorrows; and I would have gladly surrendered to his argument if he had convinced my heart as thoroughly as he did my mind.

Thus the hours slipped by and, unnoticed by me, the sky was lightening with dawn. I started as I raised my eyes and saw the glorious colours that painted the clouds to welcome the rising sun. And at that early hour, when the shadows stretch themselves to their fullest height, I was riding in the open – no cover in sight – and I was not alone. I looked at my companion and started again: it was none other than the man in grey.

He smiled at my alarm and did not give me time to speak.

"Let us pool our advantages for the time being," he said, "as sensible people do. We can always part later if we like. The road along the mountainside, although it may not have occurred to you, is the obvious one to take. You dare not go down into the valley and you hardly want to go back over the hill, as it will lead you where you have come from. My road happens to be the same as yours. I see you are greatly worried at the approach of the sun. I will lend you your shadow while we are together and you, for your part will put up with my company. Bendel is your servant no longer but I will take his place. You don't care for me much – I'm sorry about that, but you can make use of me nevertheless. The devil is not as black as they paint him. Yesterday you made me angry, it is true, but today I will bear you no grudge. I've cheered you on your way so far, you must admit; now take your shadow on trial again.

The sun had risen; there began to be people on the road and, in spite of my inner reluctance, I accepted his offer. With a smile, he dropped my shadow onto the ground; it took its place on my horse's shadow and moved cheerfully along with us. My mind was in a strange turmoil. I rode past a handful of country folk, who raised their hats and drew respectfully aside to make room for the distinguished-looking traveller. I rode on and looked sideways from time to time at what was once my shadow, which I now had only on loan from my bitterest enemy.

He walked carefree beside me, whistling a tune – he on foot, I on horseback. The temptation was irresistible; I jerked the horse's head aside, clapped on the spurs and dashed at full speed down a side road. But I could not elope with my shadow; it slid off the horse as we turned and waited by the roadside for its legal owner. Shamefaced, I was forced to come back. The man in grey finished his little tune and began to laugh.

"It will only stick to you," he said, resetting my shadow in its place, "when you have once more become its legal owner. I hold you by your shadow – you cannot escape me. A rich man like you simply cannot do without a shadow. That's fair enough – I only blame you for not having thought of it before."

I continued my journey on the same road as before. Once again, I enjoyed all the comforts and luxuries of life. I could move about freely and easily, for I had a shadow – albeit a borrowed one – and everywhere I imposed that respect which wealth commands. But despair was in my heart. My weird companion, who gave himself out as the unworthy servant of the richest man in the world, was exceedingly dexterous and clever, showing the most remarkable aptitude for his duties – in short, the model of a valet. But he never left my side, arguing with me incessantly and showing the greatest confidence that in the end I would conclude the deal over my shadow, if only to get rid of him. He was a nuisance, always hateful and at times I was really quite afraid of him; for he had made himself indispensable. I was again in his power for he had driven me back to the worldly vanities which I had abandoned. I had to suffer his eloquence and at times was almost forced to agree with him. A rich man must have a shadow in the world; and as long as I chose to maintain that station to which he had induced me to aspire, there seemed but one solution for me. But one thing I determined. Having sacrificed my love and made my life a misery, I would not transfer my soul to this being – not for all the shadows in the world. But I could not imagine how it would end.

One day we sat down in front of a cave, a local tourist attraction much frequented by travellers crossing the mountains. You could hear the roar of subterranean waters and a stone thrown into the abyss fell without echo into the immeasurable depths. Once again, he was busy painting, with extravagant flights of fancy, a glowing and colourful picture of the brilliant figure I might cut in the world by means of my purse. If only my shadow were my own again. Sitting on the ground with my elbows supported on my knees and my face hidden in my hands, I listened to the deceiver. My heart was torn between his blandishments and my own resolution. I could no longer endure my inner conflict and the decisive struggle began.

"You forget," I broke in, "that I only allowed you to stay with me on certain conditions and that I have full liberty of action still."

"I shall go if you bid me." That was his usual threat. I remained silent and he at once began to roll up my shadow. I turned pale but did not intervene. There was a long silence.

"You cannot bear me, sir," he broke out at last. "I know you hate me, but why do you hate me so? Is it because you attacked me on the highway and tried with violence to rob me of my bird's nest? Or is it because of your fraudulent attempt to get hold of my property – the shadow, which you were holding in trust? Personally, I don't hate you for all that. On the contrary, it seems quite natural to me that you should make the most of your advantage – turning your strength and cunning to good account. That you happen to have very strict principles and are honesty itself, is a hobby of yours with which I have no quarrel. My own principles are not so strict but you'll admit I'm acting according to your code. Did I ever try to strangle you in order to obtain possession of your valuable soul, to which I have really taken a great fancy? For the sake of my bartered purse, have I ever set my servant on you and tried to run away with it." I said nothing. "Well, sir," he continued, "so you cannot endure me. I can understand that and don't hold it against you. Obviously, we must part and I must admit, you are becoming very boring to me, too. But to get rid of my humiliating presence for ever, I will advise you once more – buy the thing from me."

I held out the purse. "For this?" I said.

"No."

"Well, then," I said, with a deep sigh, "I insist that we part. Do not bar my way any longer in a world which I trust is big enough for us both."

"I go," he said smiling, "but first I will show you how to ring for me, when you need the presence of your humble servant. You need only to shake your purse; the tinkle of its contents will draw me instantly to your side. Everybody thinks of his own interest in this world but you see I am thinking of yours as well. For you're getting a new power from me. Excellent purse, so even if the moths devour your shadow, it will always be a strong bond between us. But enough of this – you possess me while you possess my gold. However distant, I am at your command. You know that I am always at the disposal of my friends and that for the wealthy I have an especial regard – you've seen that for yourself. But as for your shadow, sir, let me assure you it will never be yours save on one condition alone."

Ghosts of the past floated before my eyes.

"Did Mr John give you his signature?" I asked.

"With so good a friend," he said smiling, "it was hardly necessary." "Where is he?" I demanded, "In God's name, I must know!"

Slowly he put his hand in his pocket and drew out by the hair the pale and ghastly form of Thomas John.

"*Justo Judicio Dei judicatus sum.*"* The terrible words trembled on its blue and livid lips. "*Justo Judicio Dei condemnatus sum.*"*

I was frozen with horror.

"Leave me!" I cried and flung the purse violently from me into the abyss. "I adjure you in the name of God, monster! Never let me see you again."

He rose darkly and left me. His figure seemed to vanish immediately behind the masses of savage rocks.

9

I SAT THERE PENNILESS and without my shadow, but a heavy load had dropped from my heart and I was calm. If I had not lost Mina, or if I could have ceased reproaching myself for that loss, I believe I should have been almost happy. But I did not know where to turn. I searched my pockets; a few pieces of gold were left. With a smile I counted them. My horse was at the inn below. I was ashamed to go back to fetch it – at least until the sun set. I stretched myself in the shade of a nearby tree and fell quietly asleep.

The most delightful images danced through my happy dreams. Mina, crowned with flowers, bent over me and cheered me with a loving smile. Bendel, too, was there and came towards me, wreathed with flowers and smiles to greet me warmly. There were others also and in the distant crowd I thought I could even see you, Chamisso. A bright light shone, but there were no shadows; stranger still, all appeared happy. Flowers, music, love and joy under the palmy groves. I could hardly take in – let alone distinguish or point out – the lovely forms that flitted by and as quickly vanished again; but I was happy in my dream and only wanted never to wake. I kept my eyes closed even as I was waking so that the fading dream might stay with me a little longer.

But at last I must open my eyes. The sun was still shining, but it was in the east. I had slept the whole night through. I took this for a sign that I ought not to return to the inn. Without a qualm I abandoned all my possessions, which I had left there the day before, and decided to set out on foot down a lane which led through the forest-girt base of the hill, and leave what became of me in the hands of fate. I did not look back; I never even thought of applying to Bendel, whom I had left wealthy behind me and who could so easily have helped. I began instead to think about the new role I must assume in the world. My appearance was quite unpretentious. I wore an old black coat, dating from my days in Berlin and which, for some reason, I had taken on this journey. A travelling cap was on my head and a pair of worn old boots on my feet. I stood up, cut myself a knotted stick as a kind of memento, and set off on my wanderings.

Before long, I overtook an old peasant in the wood. He greeted me kindly and we fell into conversation. Acting the curious visitor, I asked him about the way, the neighbourhood and its inhabitants, the produce of the region and so forth. He answered my questions freely and with plenty of good sense. In time we came to the bed of a mountain stream which had at one time ravaged this part of the forest. I trembled inwardly at the wide sunny stretch ahead and let the peasant walk before me. However, he stood still in the middle of the clearing and turned back towards me so as to tell me the story of the flood. He soon saw what I was lacking and stopped in the middle of his tale.

"But what's this?" he said in surprise, "the gentleman has no shadow."

"Alas," I answered with a sigh. "I have had a long and terrible illness in which I lost my hair and nails along with my shadow. Look, old man, how my hair has grown again white though I'm young and my nails are sadly short; and my shadow has not yet started to sprout again.

"Fancy." said the old man, shaking his head dubiously. "That's odd – no shadow. It must have been a sad illness indeed." But he did not go on with his story and at the next fork in the road he drifted away from me without a word of farewell. All my serenity was shattered; I could have wept.

Heavy hearted, I went on my way, seeking the company of man no longer. I hid myself in the depths of the forest and was often obliged to wait for hours before I could cross the patches of sunshine, even though there was no human eye to spy on my progress. In the dark of evening I took refuge in the villages. At last I turned my steps in the direction of a mine in the mountains, where I hoped to find employment underground: for not only was it essential that I earn my living but I could see that only the most arduous labour would distract me from my destructive thoughts.

A couple of rainy days speeded my progress but at the cost of my boots, which had been made for

Count Peter and not for pacing the by-ways like a tramp. I was soon walking barefoot and forced to buy another pair of boots. I set about this carefully next morning in the village, where a fair was in progress. For a long time I looked and bargained. I had to abandon the idea of a new pair because the price was exorbitant and made do with old ones instead. They seemed firm and strong, however, and the fair-skinned, light-haired shop boy handed them to me in return for my money with a ready smile and wished me a happy journey. I put them on immediately and left the village by its northern gate.

I was lost in thought and hardly noticed where I was going. I was still thinking about the mine, where I hoped to arrive that evening, and wondering how to present myself there. I had not walked two hundred paces when I realized that I had lost my way. I looked about me. I was in a deserted forest; no axe, it seemed, had ever been laid to the roots of those ancient firs. I hurried on a few steps and saw that only moss and stones surrounded me; piles of snow and ice lay between the dreary rocks. The wind was bitterly cold and when I looked round I saw that the forest had completely vanished. Another few paces and I seemed locked in the stillness of death. The ice on which I stood stretched endlessly before me. A dark mist hung over everything. The sun on the edge of the horizon looked like a glowing red ball. The cold was unbearable but somehow the cruel frost forced me to quicken my steps. The thunder of distant waters – another step had brought me to the ocean's ice-bound shore. Droves of seals plunged from the ice-floes into the sea. I followed the shore and saw again naked rocks, wide plains, forests of birch and pine. I advanced for a few minutes – the heat was stifling – round me were richly cultivated rice fields and groves of mulberry trees, in whose shade I sat down. I looked at my watch and found it was less than a quarter of an hour since I had left the village. I thought I must be dreaming and bit my tongue to wake myself up; but I was thoroughly awake already. Closing my eyes, I tried to collect my scattered wits. Strange foreign words, spoken in a nasal voice, fell on my ear. I turned round; two Chinese – I could not possibly mistake their Asiatic faces – were saluting me after the custom of their country and in their own tongue. I stood up and walked back a couple of steps. I could see them no longer – the landscape had changed entirely. Trees and woods had taken the place of rice fields. Looking carefully at the vegetation around me, I came to the conclusion I was in South-eastern Asia. I moved towards a tree and everything was different again. I began to march slowly forwards, like a recruit on the barrack square. A wonderful panorama of countries – fields and meadows, mountains, wastes and sandy deserts – unrolled before my astonished eyes. There could be no doubt about it – I wore the seven-league boots on my feet.

10

I FELL TO MY KNEES in an access of gratitude and devotion. Suddenly my future opened before me in glowing colours. Shut out as I was from human society by my youthful folly, the glories of nature, which I had always loved, were spread before me like a garden of unparalleled richness. These would be the objects of my study, the guide and strength of a life whose sole aim was the pursuit of science. It was not a decision that I made consciously at the time. But the bright picture that then smote my inner eye I have since tried to describe in detail, with earnest and unremitting care, and my happiness has depended on the intensity and accuracy of my recollections.

I stood up quickly, in order to make a rapid survey of the territory that would be the field of my study. I was standing on the mountains of Tibet and the sun, which I had seen rising only a few hours ago, was now sinking in the west. I covered Asia from east to west and passed the boundaries of Africa. I explored the country in great detail, crossing and recrossing it in all directions. As I gazed at the ancient pyramids and temples of Egypt, I noticed in the desert near the city of Thebes with its hundred gates, the caves once occupied by Christian hermits. It struck me forcibly that here I should live one day. I chose one of the most inconspicuous, which was at the same time roomy, convenient and inaccessible to wild beasts, to be my future home.

I moved on into Europe by the Pillars of Hercules and, after I had made a rapid survey of its southern and northern provinces, I hurried to Northern Asia and thence over the Polar Glaciers to Greenland and America. I roamed through both parts of that continent and the winter which had started in the south soon drove me back northwards from Cape Horn.

After a short rest I started on my wanderings again. I followed the mountain ranges, some of the highest in the world, through the two Americas. Slowly and prudently, I stepped from peak to peak, now over flaming volcanoes, now over snowy heights. Often I could hardly breathe at that dizzy altitude but I managed to reach Mount Elias and sprang to Asia across the Bering Straits. I followed the winding coastline, noticing specially which of the islands in the neighbourhood were accessible to me. From the Malacca peninsula my boots took me to Sumatra, Java, Bali and Lamboc. I tried, often in danger and alas, always in vain, to find a north-west passage over the inlets and rocks with which the ocean is studded, to Borneo and the other islands of the Archipelago. At last, giving up all hope, I sat down on the furthest point of Lamboc and, turning my eyes south-eastward, I mourned as if behind the bars of a prison that I could go no further. New Holland, that extraordinary country, so essential to an understanding of the structure of the earth and its vegetable and animal life, and the Antarctic South Sea with its Zoophyte Islands, were barred to me. And so the evidence on which I planned to build my scientific studies was condemned from the very first to be incomplete. Such, O Adelbert, are the limitations of man's striving.

How often, in the bitter winter of the southern hemisphere, I have started from Cape Horn, to cross the two hundred or so paces which divided me from New Holland and Van Diemen's Land, careless of how I should return or of whether that terrible land would shut down upon me like the lid of my coffin. I tried to set foot on the polar glaciers to the west and, passing perilously over the floating ice, to brave the frost and the sea. But in vain. I never reached New Holland. Each time I found myself back in Lamboc, looking longingly to the south and east, like a prisoner in his cell.

At last I abandoned this spot and with a sad heart travelled to the interior of Asia. I hurried on, seeing the day break to the west of me and by nightfall had reached my cave in the desert near Thebes, which I had left the previous afternoon.

As soon as I had had a rest and day had dawned upon Europe, I began to equip myself for my studies. First some overshoes, to act as a brake; for I had discovered that, however inconvenient it might be, the only way of shortening my pace in order to explore my surroundings in detail, was to take off my boots. A pair of overshoes produced the desired effect and later on I always carried another spare set, as I often had to abandon one pair quickly at the approach of men or wild animals while I was botanising. My excellent watch was all the timepiece I needed for the short duration of my journeys, but I also had to have a sextant, some surveying instruments and books.

To obtain these I made a few tedious journeys to London and Paris, which were both conveniently overshadowed by fog. As the rest of my magic gold was now exhausted, I took with me for payment some elephants' tusks, easily obtained in Africa, although I had to choose the smallest among them lest their weight be too much for my strength. I had soon stocked up with everything I needed and embarked on my new life as a solitary man of learning.

I travelled all over the east – measuring the mountains, the temperature of its air and waters; observing its animals and studying its plant life. I hurried from the equator to the pole – from one world to the other, comparing experience with experience. The eggs of the African ostrich or northern seabirds and fruit, especially bananas and dates from the tropical palms, provided my staple diet. Instead of my lost riches I had a good pipe for enjoyment – it took the place of human sympathy – while as an object for my affections, I had a little poodle who loved me and played the watchdog over my cave at Thebes. When I came home, laden with the spoils of my explorations, it sprang eagerly forwards to greet me, stirring my heart by its welcome and making me feel I was not quite alone in the world. But yet another adventure awaited me that was to drive me back among my fellow men once more.

11

O<small>NE DAY</small> I was working in the far north. My galoshes were drawn over my boots and I was collecting my specimens of lichen and other seaweeds. A polar bear had stolen up behind me and now suddenly confronted me on the narrow ledge of rock on which I stood. I wanted to throw off my slippers and move across to a nearby island, which I could easily reach by stepping on a rock which lifted its head above the waves. With one stride I reached the rock. I stepped forwards with the other foot and fell into the sea. In my panic, I had not noticed that the galosh was still drawn over that boot.

Stunned by the intense cold, I had the greatest difficulty in saving my life. As soon as I regained the shore, I hurried to the wastes of Libya to dry myself in the sun. In no time at all, however, the burning heat on my head made me feel so ill that I reeled back to the north again. I sought relief in rapid movement, hurrying with uncertain steps from west to east and from east to west; from the extremes of day and night, from the heat of summer to winter's hardest cold.

I do not know how long I staggered thus about the world. A burning fever shook me. I raged in delirium and in dreadful anguish realized that my senses were leaving me. I had the misfortune in my frenzy to tread on a traveller's foot. I must have hurt him, for he struck me violently. I staggered and fell.

When I came to my senses, I was lying comfortably in an excellent bed, which stood among many others in a large and good-looking room. Somebody sat by my bedside. People came and went through the room, going from bed to bed. Some of them stood before mine and I could hear that they were talking about me. They called me Number Twelve; but on the wall at the foot of my bed I could see quite distinctly a black marble slab, on which was inscribed in large golden letters, my name:

PETER SCHLEMIHL

quite correctly written; and under it, two lines of letters, of which I was too weak to make any sense. I closed my eyes again.

I heard someone reading aloud clearly and distinctly, a passage in which the name Peter Schlemihl was mentioned; but I could not make out the meaning of what was being said. I saw a kindly man and a beautiful woman dressed in black standing beside my bed. They seemed familiar to me though I did not recognize them.

Time passed and I gradually regained my strength. I was called Number Twelve, and Number Twelve because of his long beard, passed for a Jew but was none the less well cared for on that account. Nobody seemed to notice that he had no shadow. My boots, they assured me, were in safe keeping together with everything else that had been found with me and would be given back to me on my recovery. The place where I lay ill was called the *Schlemihlium;* and every day the patients were exhorted to pray for Peter Schlemihl, as the founder and benefactor of the hospital. The kindly man whom I had seen at my bedside was Bendel; the beautiful woman in black, Mina.

119

Unrecognized, I recuperated peacefully in the *Schlemihlium*. I discovered that I was in Bendel's home town where he had built this hospital with the remainder of my once ill-fated gold, dedicated in my name to the relief of the sick and suffering. Mina was a widow: Rascal's crimes had brought him to the gallows at last and deprived her of the greater part of her fortune. Her parents were dead. She lived here as a God-fearing widow, devoted to charitable works.

She stood near bed Number Twelve one day, talking to Bendel.

"Dear lady," he said, "why do you risk your health in this unwholesome air? Has fate been so hard on you that you want to die?"

"No, Mr Bendel," she said, "since I have dreamt out my long dream and found my true self, I am contented. I neither fear death nor hope for it any more. I think calmly now of the past and of the future. And you too – do you not serve your master and friend in this godly manner with quiet satisfaction and joy?"

"I do, I do, thanks be to God! Providence has been

good to us indeed. From a full cup we have drunk much bitter sorrow and much joy. What more can there be? Have we perhaps endured a testing only so that now, with wisdom and insight, we may embark on our true calling? How different that is from the way it all started. Who would want to live those days again and yet, on the whole, what a blessing it is that it happened. I cannot resist the conviction that our old friend also is better taken care of now than then."

"I think so too," answered the lovely widow, as they left me.

This conversation made a deep impression on me. But I was uncertain in my mind whether to reveal myself to them or not. In the end I made up my mind. I asked for paper and pencil.

"Your old friend," I wrote, "is faring better now than he did. And if he still does penance, at least he is reconciled to his fate."

Thereupon, as I now felt myself to be recovered, I asked for my clothes. They brought me the keys of the locker by my bed. Everything that belonged to me was there. I dressed, slung my case of botanical specimens – the northern plants were still there, I saw with delight – over my black coat. I drew on my boots, laid the note which I had written on my bed and no sooner out of the door, was well on my way back to Thebes.

As I made my way homewards along the Syrian coast – the selfsame road I had taken last time I left my cave – I saw my poor dog Figaro coming towards me. He had wanted to follow in the steps of his master, for whom he had waited so long. I stood still and called him. He sprang barking towards me in transports of innocent and extravagant joy. I tucked him under my arm, for of course he could not follow my footsteps, and brought him safely home. There I found everything in order and as my strength returned I took up once more my former avocations and way of life. Only for a whole year I avoided exposing myself to the winter's bitterest cold.

And thus, my dear Chamisso, I still live. My boots have not lost their fabulous power, as that learned work of the famous Tieckius, *De rebus gestis Pollicilli*, had given me reason to fear. But my own powers are failing, though I think I have used them to the utmost and not without fruit. I have studied more deeply than any of my predecessors, and to the furthest limits that my boots would take me, everything concerned with the earth: its surface, altitude, temperatures; the changes of its atmosphere; the manifestations of magnetic power; life in all forms, especially in the vegetable kingdom. I have published my findings, with the utmost exactitude and care, in a number of works and have also left a record of the various ideas and conclusions that I have reached. I have established the geography of Central Africa and the North Polar lands, of inner Asia and its eastern coastline. My *Historia sterpium plantarum utruisque orbis* represents a fragment of my *Flora universalis terrae*, and a link in my *Systema naturae*. In this I believe I have not only increased the number of known species by more than a third but have thrown considerable light on the general order of nature and the geography of plants. I am now busily engaged with my *Fauna*. I will take care that before my death the manuscripts are deposited with the Berlin University.

And you, my dear Chamisso, I have chosen to be the trustee of my wondrous tale which, when I have departed this life, may teach a useful lesson to many other people. Remember, my friend, while you live in the world to treasure first your shadow and then your money. But if you choose to live for your inner self alone, you will need no counsel of mine.

Notes

p. 101, *Justo Judicio Dei judicatus sum*: "I am judged by the just judgement of God" (Latin).

p. 101, *Justo Judicio Dei condemnatus sum*: "By the just judgement of God I am condemned" (Latin).

www.oneworldclassics.com